No, Baby, No!

For Junior, who inspired this book
G.N.

For Bram, Baby, Bram
All my love
Ellie x

Bloomsbury Publishing, London, Berlin, New York and Sydney

First published in Great Britain in July 2011 by Bloomsbury Publishing Plc
50 Bedford Square, London, WC1B 3DP

Text copyright © Grace Nichols 2011
Illustrations copyright © Eleanor Taylor 2011

The right of Grace Nichols to be identified as the author of this work has been
asserted by her in accordance with the Copyright, Designs and Patents Act 1988

The moral right of the illustrator has been asserted.

A CIP catalogue record of this book is available from the British Library

ISBN 978 1 4088 0299 1

All papers used by Bloomsbury Publishing are natural, recyclable products made
from wood grown in well-managed forests. The manufacturing processes
conform to the environmental regulations of the country of origin

Printed in China by Leo Paper Products, Heshan, Guangdong

3 5 7 9 10 8 6 4 2

www.bloomsbury.com

No, Baby, No!

Grace Nichols

Illustrated by Eleanor Taylor

BLOOMSBURY

LONDON OXFORD NEW YORK NEW DELHI SYDNEY

Whatever I do,
wherever I go,
it's always the same old cry:

'No,
Baby,
no!'

Creeping to the kitchen
to see what's cooking

Up goes the gate
and Dad comes
running . . .

'No, Baby, no!

Hot things can burn you in the kitchen.'

Tearing up the newspaper

Chewing bits in my mouth

Along comes Mum
and scoops it out
with a shout . . .

'No, Baby, no!
Newspapers are for reading, not for eating.'

Climbing
up Grandad
like a
mountaineer

Grabbing
at those glasses
he likes to wear . . .

'No, Baby, no.
Don't do that!
Without my specs
I'm blind as a bat.'

Reaching
for a book

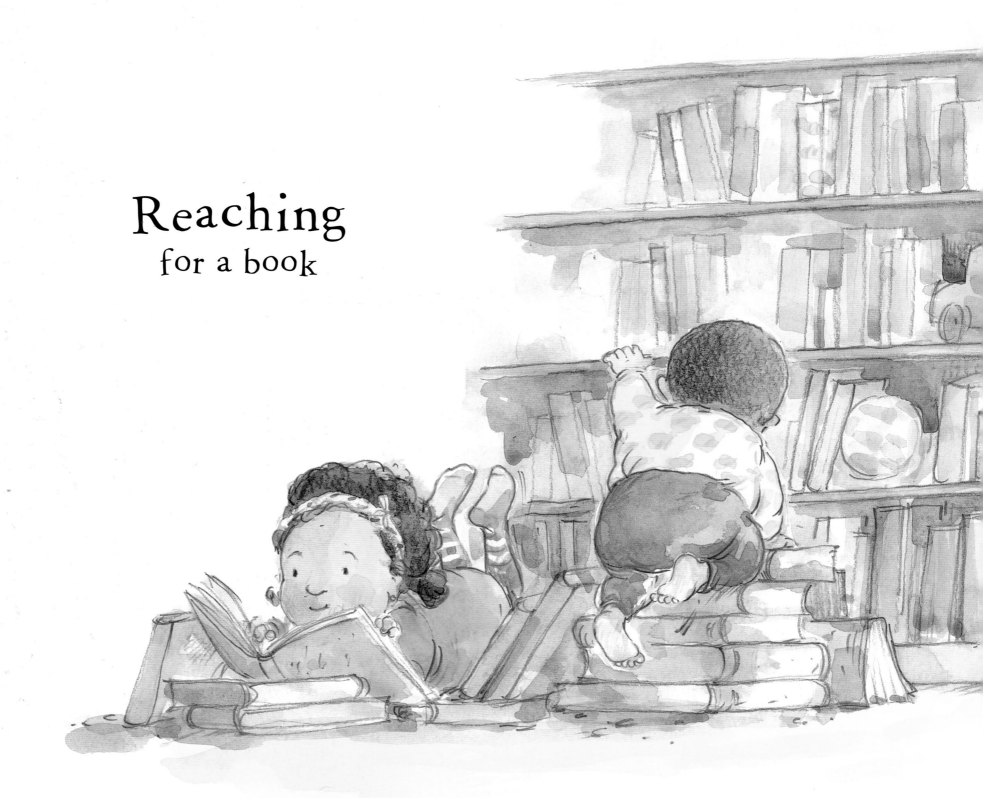

High on
a shelf

Over comes my sister
as if I need some help . . .

'No, Baby, no!
You'll pull that shelf
down on yourself.'

Having fun in the tub
with my rubber duck

Making big splashes
that go over the top . . .

'No, Baby, no!
Now Gran has to mop.'

Sitting
in my
high chair

Playing
with my mash

Again comes Mum
to feed me in a flash . . .

'No, Baby, no!

Have a taste.
Mashed potato isn't
for your face.'

Oh, **whatever** I do,
wherever I go,
it's always the same old cry:

So today
I'll try something new
with myself.

One step, two steps
. . . maybe more?

Look, I'm walking across the floor!

And no one is saying,
'No, Baby, no!'

Everyone's smiling and clapping.

'Go, Baby, go!'   'Go, Baby, go!'